FEATHER

TANGELLY

CARNELIAN

PUGSWORT

STIK

NUTBRUN

FAIRY DREAMS

*For my three gorgeous daughters who, for years, kept secret the name of
the tooth fairy and how she left her sparkly footprints on their pillows.*

Scholastic Children's Books,
Commonwealth House, 1-19 New Oxford Street,
London WC1A 1NU, UK
a division of Scholastic Ltd

London ~ New York ~ Toronto ~ Sydney ~ Auckland
Mexico City ~ New Delhi ~ Hong Kong

First published in Australia by Omnibus Books,
part of the Scholastic Group, 1999
This edition published in the UK by Scholastic Ltd, 2000

Carol McLean-Carr's artwork has been created digitally on an IBM computer. Carol outlines and scans each drawing,
and also scans textures and real objects. The drawings are rendered with a digital airbrush and each image and character is
made into a separate file. Backgrounds are sketched and scanned, then painted in Photoshop and Fractal Painter.
Finally all the files are assembled, layer on layer, and Carol begins the painstaking work of blending edges, adjusting focus
and lighting, and creating shadows and highlights.

Acknowledgement
Thanks to Steve Parish for permission to use his flora photography as resource for the illustration on pp 12-13.

FAIRY DREAMS

Written and illustrated by
Carol McLean-Carr

SCHOLASTIC
PRESS

When day is done and children dream,
The interfering fairies scheme
To move things *here* that stood right *there*,
Creating chaos everywhere.

Among these pages, hidden well,
Are toys and treasures Isobel
Has left unguarded round her room.
Now fairies come with twilight's gloom.

Her ball, her fan, her pot for tea,
The egg she found beside a tree,
Her unicorn, a pearly shell,
Her poem on the windowsill,
A bug, a box, a book, a wand,
The ship she floated on the pond:
Three times four – a fairy number,
And fairies fly as children slumber.

The fairies only mean to borrow,
And bring these treasures back tomorrow
(Some magic dust will make them small,
Playthings for the Fairies' Ball),
But as they swoop in happy play
They lose them, laugh, and fly away.

Now you must find each thing they've lost
Before the sun melts morning frost.

Chattering, squabbling fairy thieves
Float lightly in, like autumn leaves.

Turn the pages, and you'll see
How careless fairy folk can be!

Through woodland garden fairies play,
And scare the cats along the way,

But they've forgotten something blue.
A bird is looking for it too.

A ladybug of painted metal
Can look just like a fallen petal.

In a glade of fruit and flowers
A bug may lose itself for hours.

Airy bubbles float on high
And water fairies watch them fly.

The crystal ball is left behind
For other fairy folk to find.

Deep underground a dragon dreams
Of gems in boxes, gold that gleams.

A box may look like any other –
But stay away from dragon mother!

High in her tower a sorceress tells
Of magic lands and wondrous spells.

She spreads her books across the floor –
Untidy fairies leave one more.

Ships may sail upon the seas,
And some explore the galaxies,

But one is lost – drops like a stone
And never makes its way back home.

Inside a sea-cave lit with gems
Mermaids pause to splash with friends.

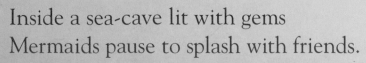

A dragon rising from the deep
Will find another shell to keep.

Magic silver horses play
In misty glades at close of day,

But one looks on, and longs to be
Among the fun beneath the tree.

It's almost time! Come one, come all!
Make ready for the Fairies' Ball!

As music spills across the land,
A wand falls from a fairy hand.

From land and sea, by silvery light,
To Faerie Tree all come tonight.

The golden doorway opens wide.
Alas, a fan is left outside.

It's time for some to stop and eat:
The kitchen's where they like to meet.

A feast of cakes and pots of tea
Can all be found in Faerie Tree.

Pipes and horns play music sweet
For flying, festive fairy feet,

And here a poem softly falls,
Forever lost in fairy halls.

Fairy dreams are things of night
And vanish with the morning light,
Yet Isobel awakes to find
Twelve gifts the fairies left behind.

CRYSTABEAU

PAMBLE

FAIRLIE

NUTTLE

BISTED

LOBELIA

TWITTER